I0799752

Rabbits Are Fun!

Mary Elizabeth Salzmann

Consulting Editor, Diane Craig, M.A./Reading Specialist

Sandcastle

An Imprint of Abdo Publishing
abdobooks.com

abdobooks.com

Published by Abdo Publishing, a division of ABDO, PO Box 398166, Minneapolis, Minnesota 55439. Copyright © 2022 by Abdo Consulting Group, Inc. International copyrights reserved in all countries. No part of this book may be reproduced in any form without written permission from the publisher. SandCastle™ is a trademark and logo of Abdo Publishing.

Printed in the United States of America, North Mankato, Minnesota

052021
092021

THIS BOOK CONTAINS RECYCLED MATERIALS

Design: Sarah DeYoung, Mighty Media, Inc.
Production: Mighty Media, Inc.
Cover Photograph: iStockphoto
Interior Photographs: Shutterstock (all)

Library of Congress Control Number: 2019957662

Publisher's Cataloging-in-Publication Data
Names: Salzmann, Mary Elizabeth, author.
Title: Rabbits are fun! / by Mary Elizabeth Salzmann
Description: Minneapolis, Minnesota : Abdo Publishing, 2022 | Series: Pets are fun! | Includes online resources and index
Identifiers: ISBN 9781532193149 (lib. bdg.) | ISBN 9781098211783 (ebook)
Subjects: LCSH: Pets--Juvenile literature. | Rabbits--Juvenile literature. | Rabbits--Behavior--Juvenile literature. | Pets--Behavior--Juvenile literature.
Classification: DDC 636.08--dc23

SandCastle™ Level: Emerging

SandCastle™ books are created by a team of professional educators, reading specialists, and content developers around five essential components—phonemic awareness, phonics, vocabulary, text comprehension, and fluency—to assist young readers as they develop reading skills and strategies and increase their general knowledge. All books are written, reviewed, and leveled for guided reading and early reading intervention programs for use in shared, guided, and independent reading and writing activities to support a balanced approach to literacy instruction. The SandCastle™ series has four levels that correspond to early literacy development. The levels are provided to help teachers and parents select appropriate books for young readers.

EMERGING • BEGINNING • TRANSITIONAL • FLUENT

Contents

Rabbits Are Fun!

Can you find these pet rabbits in this book?

Dutch

English Lop

English Spot

Flemish Giant

Holland Lop

Lionhead

Look at the rabbit's ears.

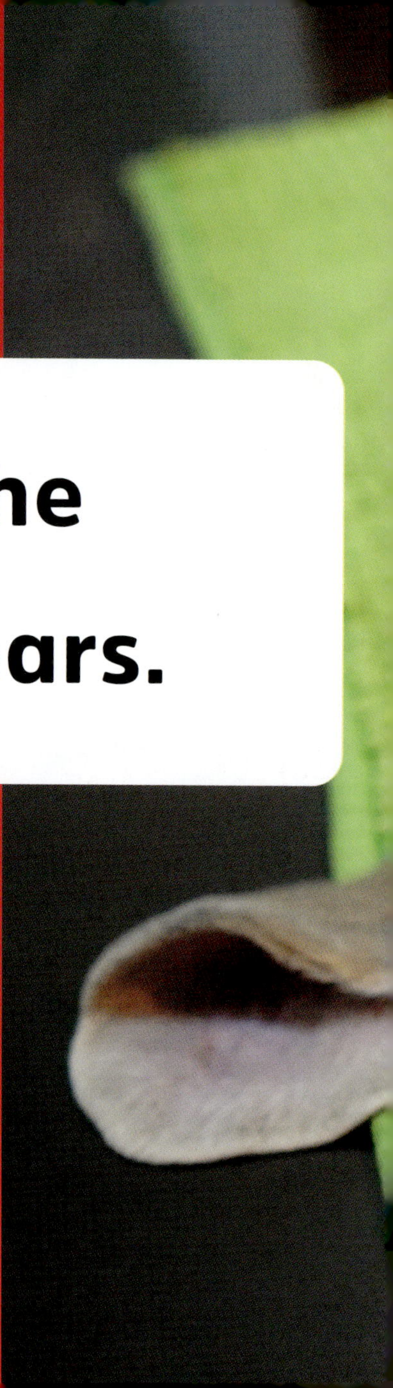

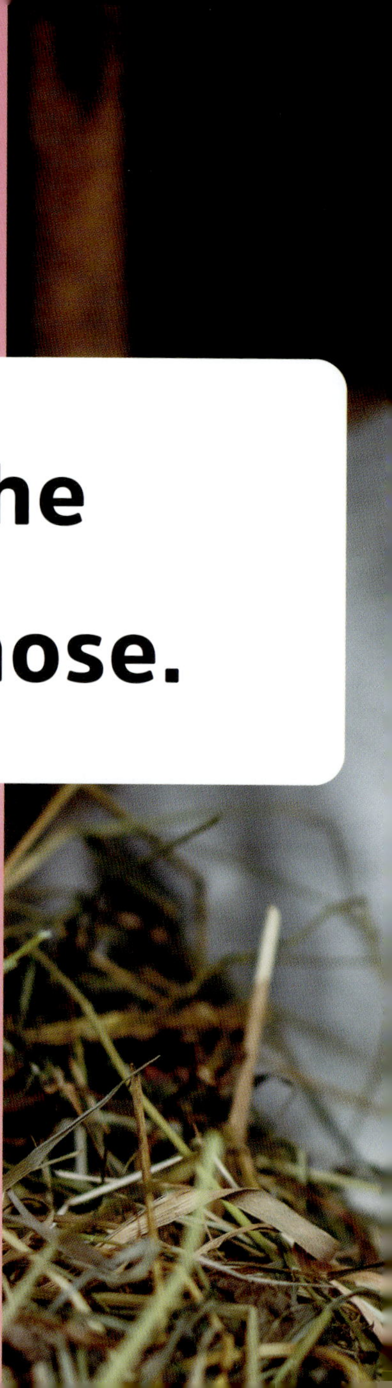

Look at the rabbit's nose.

Look at the rabbit's spots.

Look at the rabbit's hair.

Look at the rabbit's feet.

Look at the rabbit's bed.

Look at the rabbit's food.

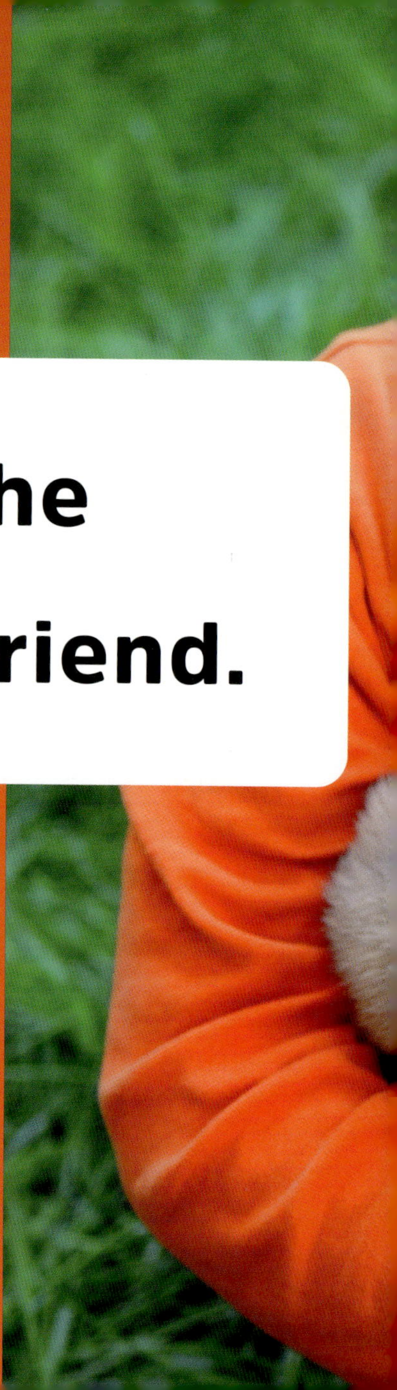

Look at the rabbit's friend.

What Else Did You See?

flower

hay

leaves

rug

Index

Teacher's Guide

ATOS: 0.7 GRL: A Word Count: 40

High-Frequency Words

at look the

Content Words

bed, ears, feet, food, friend, hair, nose, rabbit, spots

Before Reading

- Tell students that the title of the book is *Rabbits Are Fun!*
- Summarize the content of the book.
- Have students look through the book. Ask them what they see in the pictures.
- Choose a few new vocabulary words. Have students predict what letter each word starts with. Then have them find the words in the book.

After Reading

Ask students questions about the book's content, such as:

- Have you ever held or petted a rabbit? What was it like?
- Do you have a pet? What kind of pet is it?
- What other animals would you like to read about?